SECRETS OF THE LIBRARY OF DOOM

THE PUZZLER'S RIDDLES

BY MICHAEL DAHL
ILLUSTRATED BY PATRICIO CLAREY

Raintree is an imprint of Capstone Global Library Limited, a company
incorporated in England and Wales having its registered office at 264
Banbury Road, Oxford, OX2 7DY – Registered company number: 6695582

www.raintree.co.uk
myorders@raintree.co.uk

Designed by Hilary Wacholz
Original illustrations © Capstone Global Library Limited 2022
Originated by Capstone Global Library Ltd

978 1 3982 2374 5

British Library Cataloguing in Publication Data
A full catalogue record for this book is available from the British Library.

CONTENTS

The Library of Doom is a hidden fortress.
It holds the world's largest collection
of strange and dangerous books.

Behold the Librarian. He defends the Library – and
the world – from super-villains, clever thieves
and fierce monsters. Many of his adventures
have remained secret. Now they can be told.

SECRET #87

EACH BOOK IS ITS OWN PUZZLE,
BUT NOT ALL CAN BE SOLVED.

Chapter One

WRONG TURN

A school bus drives **QUICKLY** through a city at night.

The three students inside are **SHOUTING**.

"This is the **WRONG** turn!" they yell.

"We're here!" says the bus driver.

SQUUUEEEEEEAAK!

The bus stops suddenly.

"Where is *here*?" asks a girl named Spring. "This isn't home."

The driver **OPENS** the door and hops out. The students follow.

A STRANGE-LOOKING park stretches before them.

The bus driver stands on a path of yellow bricks.

An archway rises above the path. **SHINY** letters on it say:

PUZZLE

PARK

"See that bus?" the driver asks. He points to a yellow **SPECK** far away. "I've *booked* you a trip home, if you can reach it!"

The man grins. "Follow the path and solve the **RIDDLES**, or stay here forever!"

Then the bus driver disappears in a puff of smoke.

Chapter Two

PUZZLE PATH

"Who was that guy really?" asks the boy Tripp.

"Let's just get to that bus," says Gamble, the other boy.

The students **FOLLOW** the brick path.

Spring stops. "Um, is that a flock of sheep?"

Sheep are NIBBLING grass nearby.

Then their wool becomes **DARKER**. Their teeth grow longer and sharper.

"No, those are wolves in sheep's clothing!" shouts Gamble.

The wolves **CREEP** towards the kids.

Spring points to the bricks **BENEATH** her feet.

"Look," she says. "There are words on the path."

WHAT LETTERS ARE FOUND IN A FLOCK OF SHEEP?

"It's a riddle, like the driver said," says Tripp. "But what's the answer?"

The wolves **POUNCE**.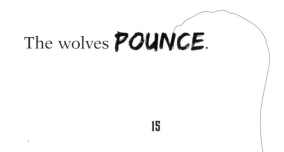

Chapter Three

YOU CHOOSE

Spring **SHOUTS**, "Ewes!"

The wolves instantly turn **BACK** into fluffy sheep.

"Get it?" Spring asks. "*Ewe* is the word for a female sheep. It sounds just like the letter *U*."

"I just want to get out of here!"
says Gamble.

"Oh no!" says Tripp. He **POINTS**
ahead.

The yellow road splits into three
different paths. Each path leads to
a long, rickety bridge. Each bridge
crosses over a **BOTTOMLESS** pit.

"It's another puzzle," says Gamble.

Behind them, bunnies hop out of the trees. But like the sheep, the bunnies are not what they seem.

Their eyes **GLOW** blood-red. They have dripping fangs.

"Hurry!" says Tripp. "Those bunnies look hopping mad!"

"But which bridge do we pick?" asks Gamble.

Just then, a wooden sign **POPS** up in front of the kids. It says:

WHICH BRIDGE IS THE RIGHT ONE? YOU CHOOSE.

"The bunnies are getting closer!" says Spring.

Chapter Four

TEDDY SCARE

Gamble grabs his friends' hands. "This way!" he **SHOUTS**.

"How do you know?" yells Tripp.

Gamble **PULLS** them across one of the bridges.

From the **PIT** below, the kids hear the roar of a troll. But the bridge does not break.

The bunnies do **NOT** follow.

"It was the right bridge," says Gamble, "because it was the bridge on the *right side*!"

"Look!" says Tripp. "We're **SO** close!"

The bus home is just ahead of them.

CRAAAACKKKK!

Suddenly, the yellow bricks CRUMBLE beneath the students' feet.

The three friends fall into a **DEEP**, dark hole.

They land in a room with four **STONE** walls.

The bus driver is standing in front of them.

But he now wears a suit that looks like a *JIGSAW* puzzle.

"You again!" **SHOUTS** Spring.

"Call me . . . the Puzzler!" says the villain.

The Puzzler laughs. "Are you enjoying my Picture Book Puzzle Park?" he asks.

"Picture Book? That explains all the cuddly **MONSTERS**," says Spring.

"Yeah, what's next?" asks Gamble.
"An **EVIL** teddy bear?"

"Close," the Puzzler says with grin.
"I call him my Teddy *Scare*!"

One of the stone walls slides away.
A **GIANT** teddy bear stomps out of
the shadows.

Chapter Five

FINAL ANSWER

The huge teddy bear **CHOMPS** its mouth. It moves closer to the kids.

"But what's the riddle?" Tripp shouts.

"Who says there has to be one?" asks the Puzzler. "My FUZZY friend is hungry!"

Just then, a stone wall **BURSTS** open.

Bricks fly inwards. They hit the bear and rip its fabric.

Then a **TALL** man steps through the hole in the wall.

He wears **HEAVY** boots and a long coat.

The Puzzler shakes his fist. "There's no place in my book for you, Librarian!"

"I can always find my place," says the Librarian. "I use a bookmark, remember?"

The hero pulls a bookmark from his coat. He **THROWS** it towards the three kids.

The bookmark gets bigger and bigger. It GROWS to the size of a rug.

"Jump on!" the Librarian tells the kids.

The hero **LEAPS** onto the bookmark as well. It lifts up into the air.

"You forget," the Librarian yells to the Puzzler, "a teddy bear is never hungry!"

The Puzzler **SCRATCHES** his head. "Why?" he asks.

"Because it's *stuffed*," says the hero.

Stuffing suddenly **SPILLS** out from the giant, ripped teddy bear.

The Puzzler is quickly **BURIED** beneath piles of fluff.

"We'll let the Puzzler solve *that* problem," says the Librarian.

The kids cheer as the bookmark **SOARS** out of the room and towards home.

GLOSSARY

book to get something for future use, such as buying tickets for a trip

creep to move slowly

cuddly having a cute, soft or likeable look

ewe a female sheep

fang a sharp tooth an animal uses to grab and tear its food

nibble to take small bites

pounce to jump quickly at something, often in order to catch it

rickety shaky and likely to fall apart at any moment

riddle a question or statement that is meant to be tricky to work out

stuffed filled with a soft material; also, filled with food and no longer hungry

TALK ABOUT IT

1. How do you think the children felt when they found out they needed to solve puzzles to get home? What makes you think that? How would you have felt?

2. Were you surprised that the bus driver was a villain? Look at the start of the story again. What clues are there that he isn't a normal driver?

WRITE ABOUT IT

1. Imagine the Librarian didn't burst into the room to stop the Puzzler. How do the kids escape the Teddy Scare? Write a new ending!

2. Picture Book Puzzle Park is full of things that seem cute and friendly, but really aren't. There are wolves, evil bunnies and hungry teddy bears. What else might be in the park? Describe the creatures.

ABOUT THE AUTHOR

Michael Dahl is an award-winning author of more than 200 books for young people. He especially likes to write scary or weird fiction. His latest series are the sci-fi adventure Escape from Planet Alcatraz and School Bus of Horrors. As a child, Michael spent lots of time in libraries. "The creepier, the better," he says. These days, besides writing, he likes travelling and hunting for the one, true door that leads to the Library of Doom.

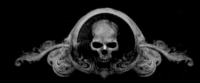

ABOUT THE ILLUSTRATOR

Patricio Clarey was born in Argentina. He graduated in fine arts from the Martín A. Malharro School of Visual Arts, specializing in illustration and graphic design. Patricio currently lives in Barcelona, Spain, where he works as a freelance graphic designer and illustrator. He has created several comics and graphic novels, and his work has been featured in books and other publications.